HOGS HATE HUGS!

The best hugs are the ones we share…
T. B-B. & J. B-B.

Published by Lion Children's Books
an imprint of
Lion Hudson plc
Wilkinson House, Jordan Hill Road,
Oxford OX2 8DR, England
www.lionhudson.com/lionchildrens

Hardback ISBN 978 0 7459 6514 7
Paperback ISBN 978 0 7459 6483 6

First edition 2014

A catalogue record for this book is available from the British Library

Printed and bound in Malaysia, December 2014, LH18

HOGS HATE HUGS!

Tiziana Bendall-Brunello
Illustrated by John Bendall-Brunello

LION
CHILDREN'S

Little Hog was just a bit fed up. You see, he was always having to hug everyone – because he was the *cutest cuddliest little hog* in the whole forest.

When he got up, Mummy Hog always gave him a long morning hug.

And if he ever hurt himself…

Daddy Hog would hold Little Hog in a
DADDY-SIZED HUG.

Even when he went to see his friends,
it was the same thing –

there were BIG hugs with Bear

and small hugs with Mouse…

S l o o o o o w hugs with Turtle

and hopping-quick hugs with Rabbit.

But his little sister was the worst. She made him stand with his arms wide open and she would rush at him as fast as her little legs would carry her and…

OOMMPH!

Down they went!

She always wanted to give Little Hog

a r u n n i n g - f l y i n g h u g .

One day, after a prickly hug with Hedgehog

and a **heavy** hug with Badger,

Little Hog decided he'd had enough.

"I HATE hugs!" said Little Hog.

"Oh! But you're so huggable," said Owl as she grabbed Little Hog with her wings and gave him a tickly hug.

"No! NO, I'm not!" shouted Little Hog. "Now leave me alone!"

"I'm too old for all this hugging!" shouted Little Hog.
And he sat down and made a poster.

Then he nailed it to the Big Tree right where everyone
could see it.

"HOGS HATE HUGS!" it said in big letters – and it
was signed *Little Hog*.

And he stomped off into the forest.

Not long after that, all the animals gathered around the tree to read the poster – and they were all shocked. Didn't Little Hog want to be hugged any more? Did he REALLY think that he was getting too old for hugging?

"You can never be too old for a good hug!" said Owl, and all the others agreed.

Everyone went quiet. But just then Mouse had an idea…

She whispered into
Mummy Hog's ear, and
before too long Mummy
Hog came back with
something.

By this time it had started to get dark in the forest, and Little Hog was beginning to feel a bit lonely and a bit afraid.

Then he heard a strange shuffling sound coming from just behind him.

He span around and got a horrible shock. It looked like
a **GHOSTLY MONSTER** coming towards him!

What could it be? Little Hog didn't wait to find out.

He started to run and run.

But then the monster tripped over!

Little Hog turned around to look – and there
were all his friends and his Mummy.

"Do you still hate hugs?" asked Mummy Hog.
"Or do you need just a little hug after all?"

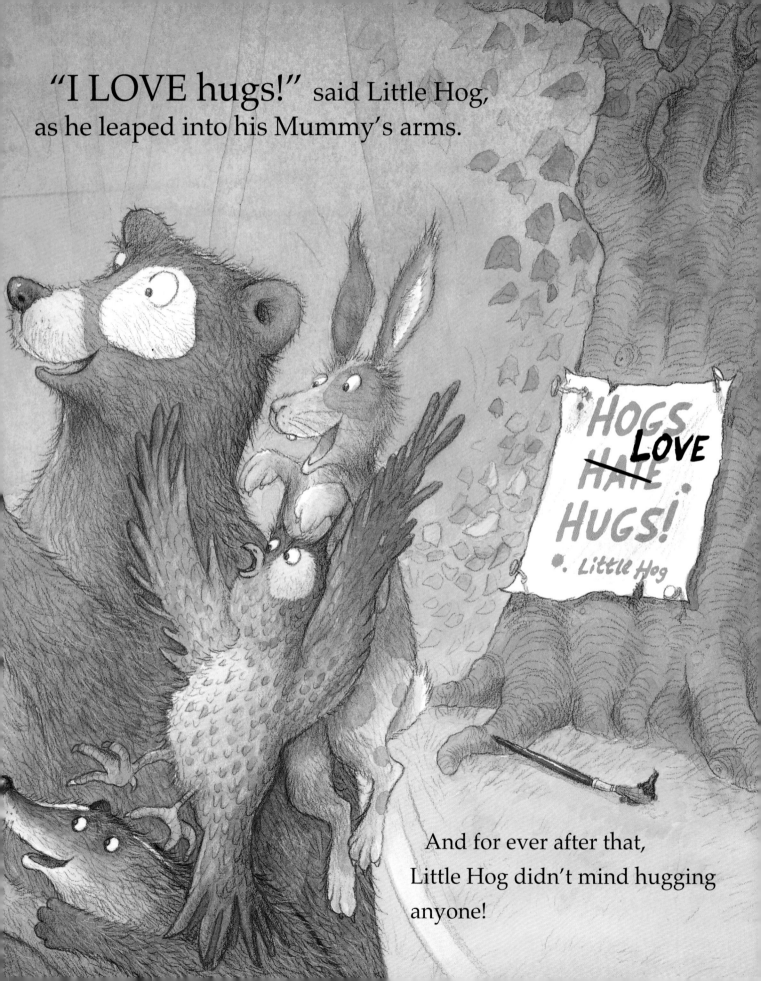

"I LOVE hugs!" said Little Hog,
as he leaped into his Mummy's arms.

HOGS ~~HATE~~ LOVE HUGS!
•. Little Hog

And for ever after that,
Little Hog didn't mind hugging
anyone!

Other titles from Lion Children's Books

Are You Sad, Little Bear?   *Rachel Rivett & Tina Macnaughton*
The Biggest Thing in the World   *Kenneth Steven & Melanie Mitchell*
Zoo Girl   *Rebecca Elliott*